Based on The Railway Series by the Rev. W. Awdry.

Written by Christopher Awdry
© William Heinemann Limited 1992

Cover illustration by Owain Bell
© Britt Allcroft (Thomas) Limited 1991

Endpaper illustration by Owain Bell
© Britt Allcroft (Thomas) Limited 1992

Illustration on pages 58-59 by Owain Bell
© Britt Allcroft (Thomas) Limited 1992

Photographic stills by David Mitton and Terry Permane for Britt Allcroft's
production of "Thomas the Tank Engine and Friends" © Britt Allcroft (Thomas)
Ltd 1991, 1992

Other full colour illustrations by Primary Design.
Line work by David Palmer (Temple Rogers).
© Britt Allcroft (Thomas) Limited 1992.

Published by
GRANDREAMS LIMITED
Jadwin House
205/211 Kentish Town Road
London
NW5 2JU

Printed in Belgium

ISBN 0 86227 957 7

CONTENTS

Hello!

I say, I'm very flattered! I didn't expect the Fat Controller to ask me to think of an introduction to this year's Thomas the Tank Engine and Friends Annual. After all, I'm not one of his engines, though I like to think I'm one of Thomas's friends.

Anyway, the Fat Controller came to my garage the other day and told my driver that there was going to be a story about me in the new Annual, so did he think I might like to introduce the whole book. Well, you don't think I needed asking twice do you?

As well as the story about Thomas and me and the very important visitor, there's one about Gordon's near miss. And there is also a story about Oliver and a parrot called Cocky. Oliver hasn't been with us long, and I don't know him very well yet, but I know you'll like him. Fancy being fooled by a bird!

As always, there's lots more entertainment in Thomas's Annual besides the stories, so I won't waste any more of your time. Good reading.

One morning as James waited to leave the Big Station, the Fat Controller came to see him.

"I hope that you can give us a good run this morning, James," he said. "I have an important meeting to go to, and I don't want to be late. Do your best, won't you."

"Of course, Sir," replied James. "We'll have you there in no time."

"Well done," laughed the Fat Controller. "I know I can rely on you."

On every passenger train there is something called an emergency cord. If there is an emergency it can be used to call the Guard, and it automatically stops the train at the same time. But it must only be used in an emergency, otherwise the person who pulled it may have to pay a fine.

On James's train today there was a party of foreign holiday makers. They could not understand English very well, and thought that the chain above the door was for calling the buffet car attendant. So they pulled it - suddenly the brakes came on and James had to stop as quickly as he could.

"Oh no," he groaned as he came to a standstill. "Now what?"

8

S TRAFFIC JAM

"Emergency, James," said his driver, looking back. "Someone has pulled the emergency communication cord."

The Guard walked along the train to find out what was wrong. The foreign visitors were pleased to see him, but the Guard was not pleased when they asked him for four cups of coffee!

The matter was soon cleared up, and the Guard told James he could go. But when he

tried to start, he found that he couldn't. The sudden action of the brakes had locked them solid and James couldn't move an inch.

What was worse, the train had stopped right across a level crossing, and by now there were long queues of cars on both sides waiting to get over the railway. James was overcome with embarrassment, but he couldn't do a thing about it.

The Fat Controller came, and the motorists all told him what a nuisance the railway was.

"I'm sorry, Sir," said James sadly.

"Not your fault, James," he replied, "but I don't know how I'm going to reach my meeting."

James didn't either. Then a flash of colour in the traffic queue caught his eye.

"Isn't that Bertie waiting?" he said. "Maybe he can turn around and..."

In a flash James's fireman was running down the road. A few

minutes later he came back grinning broadly.

"No problem, Sir," he said to the Fat Controller. "He's trying to reach the same place as you. He says he'll be happy to take you when he has turned."

It was another hour before a fitter came to mend the brakes, and longer still before James could get his train moving. He was very sorry, and so were the foreign visitors, but they promised not to make the same mistake again. James felt certain they wouldn't.

BREAKFAST
WITH THE FAT CONTROLLER

WHICH TWO PICTURES ARE IDENTICAL?

ANSWERS ON PAGES 60-61

COPY AND COLOUR

Copy the picture of Bertie in the grid below and then colour it in.

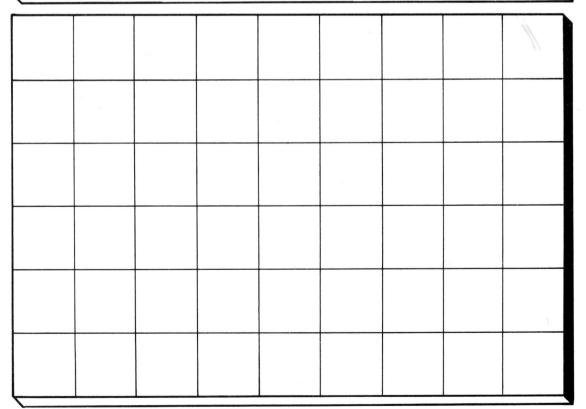

Can you find ten mice hidden in this picture?

Which engine can reach the shed?

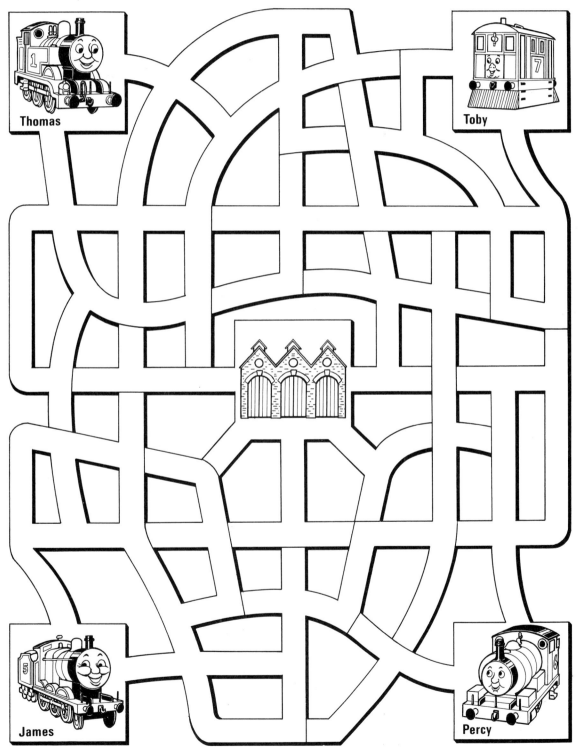

ANSWERS ON PAGES 60-61

THOMAS AND THE SNOW BLOCK

It was winter. Heavy dark clouds filled the sky. That night snow fell, and deep drifts piled up in the surrounding countryside.

Next morning Bertie the bus set out early from his garage to collect passengers for Thomas's early morning train. Thomas had hardly got Annie and Clarabel ready before they saw Bertie drive into the station yard. No passengers got out.

"We can't get over the hill," Bertie said. "People said it's not so bad on the other side of the hill, but up on top there are drifts higher than my roof. We were lucky to be able to turn around. You'll need to go steady at the tunnel, Thomas, I expect the snow is deep there too."

Just then a taxi drove into the station yard and came to a stop beside Bertie. An important looking man got out and the Stationmaster came to meet him. They went off together towards the office. Then Percy, who had been trying to take some trucks to the harbour, came back pushing them.

"The snow is deep near the tunnel," he warned them. "The

cutting is nearly full of it - I couldn't get through even with my snowplough."

"Never mind, Thomas," said his driver. "You are heavier than Percy, so perhaps we can force our way through."

They set off, but when they reached the cutting they found that the snow was so thick that it bent the snow plough, which began to damage the rails.

"That's torn it," said Thomas's driver. "We'll never get through now."

They took the snowplough

off, left it beside the line and went back to the station. Thomas took Annie and Clarabel to their shed and had just got back to the platform when the Stationmaster came up with the important looking man.

"This gentleman has to see Mr Kyndley," he said. "It is a very important matter and he must see him today at all costs."

Thomas's driver scratched his head.

"Well, I'm blowed if I know how," he said. "The road is impassable and we can't get through a cutting blocked with snow."

"A bulldozer would be handy," remarked the Fireman.

"What about Terence?" suggested Thomas. "Hasn't he got one of those pusher things that fits in front?"

"Well done Thomas!" exclaimed his driver, and the Stationmaster ran back to his office to telephone.

Meanwhile, Toby had brought Henrietta to the platform, and workmen were loading their tools into her. By the time Toby

had taken them as far as he could go into the cutting, Terence was already at work.

They were hard at it all morning, but by lunchtime they had the line clear. Toby brought the man back to Ffarquhar and told everyone at the station the good news. Then, with the very important visitor in Henrietta, and with Thomas coupled to the front

and Toby at the back, a special train set off.

Deep walls of snow stood like cliffs on either side of the lines that Terence and the railway workers had cleared, and the two engines puffed triumphantly between them. Through the tunnel they went. Bertie had been quite right, for when they came out into daylight at the other end they found that the snow lay much less thickly on this side of the hill.

The stationmaster had telephoned to warn Mr Kyndley that a special train was on its way, and he was waiting for them at the end of his garden. Thomas and Toby whistled cheerfully to him as they stopped outside the cottage, just beyond the end of the tunnel.

The Guard and the fireman cleared snow from the side of the cutting and when all was safe the Guard helped the very important visitor down from Henrietta. Both Mr Kyndley and his visitor came to

thank the engines. The Guard
walked to the house with them to
make sure they did not slip on the
path, and then Thomas and Toby,
cold but happy, left for the
junction.

When the Fat Controller
heard about the adventure, he
was pleased too. He made a
special journey to Ffarquhar to
see the engines.

"I've said it before and I'll
say it again," he told them. "There
can be no doubt that Thomas,
Toby and Percy are all Really
Useful Engines."

"And Terence and Bertie
too?" asked Percy.

"Terence and Bertie too,"
agreed the Fat Controller.

SPOT THE DIFFERENCE

Can you find ten things missing in the lower picture?

COPY AND COLOUR

Copy the picture of Terence in the grid below and then colour it in.

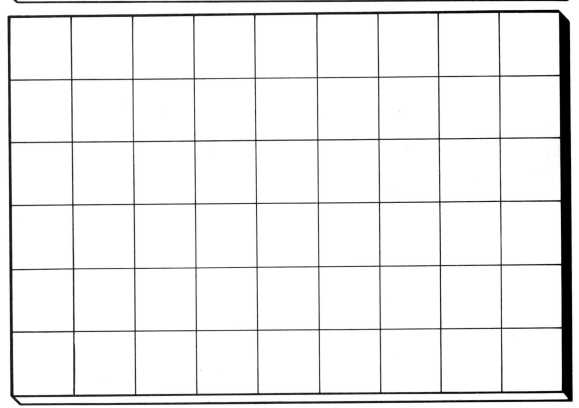

HENRY'S FOREST

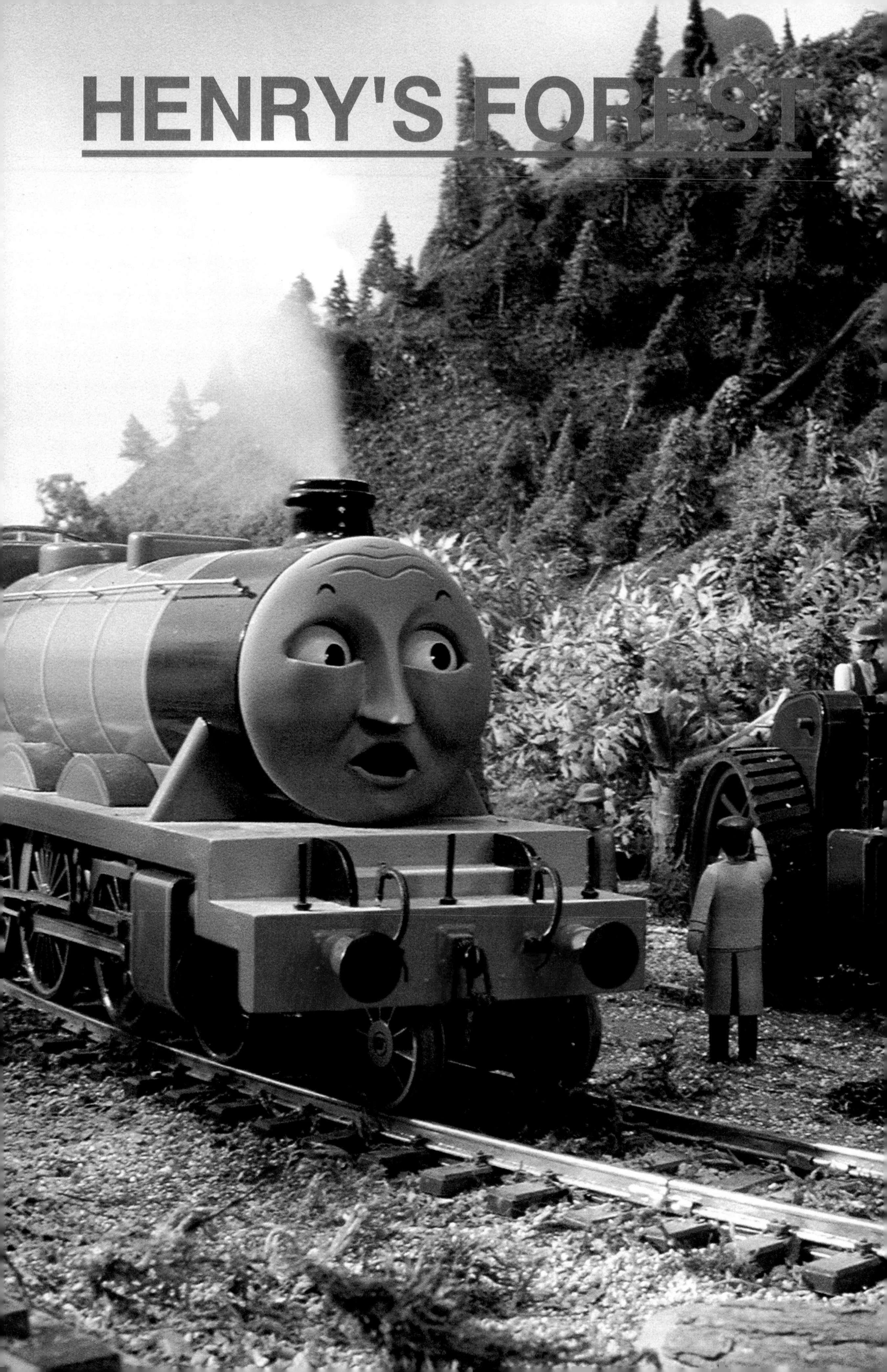

HAROLD COMES
TO THE RESUE

Oliver is a Great Western Engine. He was found by Douglas escaping from scrap with his brake van, Toad. With the help of his driver and firemen, Douglas brought Oliver and Toad to the safety of the Fat Controller's Railway.

Here they were cleaned and Oliver was painted in splendid Great Western green. All the engines and the Fat Controller were glad of the extra help Oliver could offer. Now he helps Duck to run his branch

line on the Fat Controller's railway.

One day while Oliver was waiting at the station which the other engines shared with the Small Railway, he noticed a metal cage hanging outside the Stationmaster's house. Inside the cage fluttered a brightly coloured creature.

"It's blue and green," he told Duck in the shed that night, "and it's got a yellow pointed nose, with a sort of funnel thing on top of its head. My driver said that it

talks," he added doubtfully.

"Talks!" scoffed Duck. "Why doesn't it ask to come out of its cage then?"

Duck's driver overheard them.

"It's a parrot," he laughed. "Your driver was quite right, Oliver. Some parrots can talk and this is one of them. It belongs to the Stationmaster's father - the old man was a sailor who brought the parrot back from foreign lands."

The parrot's name was Cocky. He was only put outside on fine days of course, but he quickly became a favourite with the railway staff. He didn't seem to mind the sudden noises that the engines made either. Duck and Oliver listened carefully whenever they had the chance, but try as they might they never heard Cocky say a single word.

"I don't believe he can talk," Duck said to Oliver one night. All that silly bird does is shriek and flap about." Duck was cross

because Oliver had been teasing him about the time when Donald's driver and fireman had once put a duck egg under Duck's bunker. Birds just meant trouble as far as Duck was concerned.

A few days later, Oliver was waiting for the last train on the Small Railway. It was late and Oliver was becoming impatient. When it did arrive at last, the passengers got quickly into Oliver's coaches. Oliver waited for the Guard to blow his whistle and wave his green flag.

Soon the whistle sounded but the platform was empty except for Cocky, fluttering in his cage.

"The Guard must be in his van already," the driver said. "Away we go Oliver - let's see if we can make up some of the lost time."

They had a good run, but when they reached the Big Station the Guard came up to Oliver. He looked cross.

"Whatever were you up to, rushing off like that, Oliver?" he

demanded. "Next time wait for my whistle before you start, please - you might have caused an accident."

Oliver looked puzzled.

"I'm sorry Guard," he said, "but there *was* a whistle."

"That's right," agreed his driver. "We all heard it."

Now the Guard was puzzled too!

"But I was in my van when you started," he said. "I was stacking some boxes, and you made them fall over when you dashed off like that."

Suddenly a grin spread across the Fireman's face.

"It's that Cocky!" he exclaimed. "He must have learned how to imitate the Guard's whistle!"

They soon found out he was right.

"Well, well," chuckled Duck knowingly when he heard about the confusion. "Fancy getting fooled by a bird, eh, Oliver? With my egg and your parrot, I think that makes us quits, don't you?"

A PICTURE TO PAINT

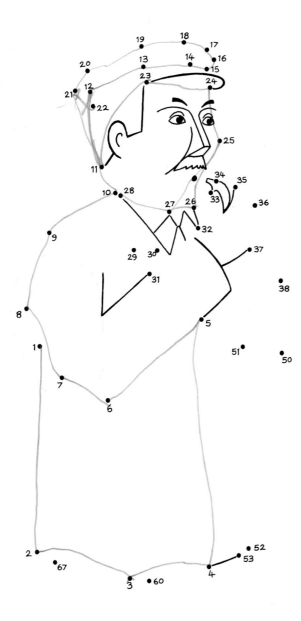

Can you find the five circled areas in the picture?

Can you help Bill find Ben through the maze?

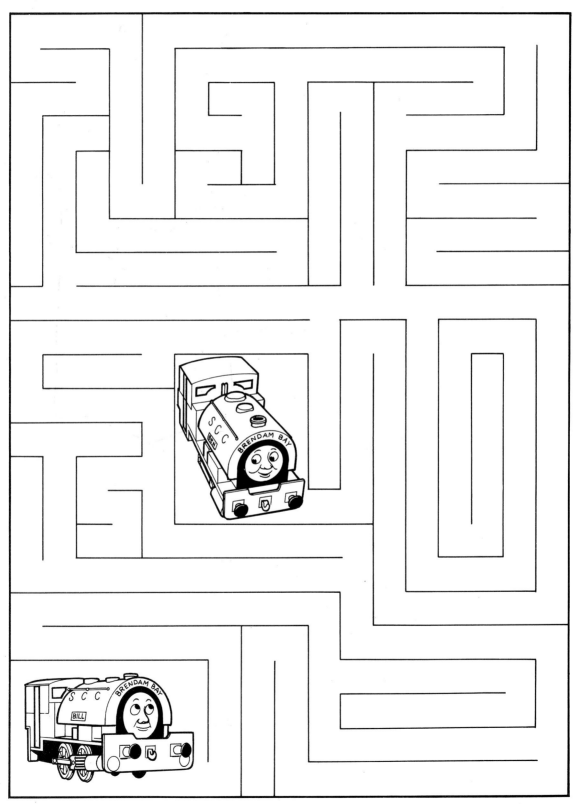

ANSWERS ON PAGES 60-61

The big engines looked anxiously at each other as the wind whistled round their engine shed.

"Driver says it will get worse before morning," said Henry gloomily.

"I remember once when a wind like this blew down the signals at the Junction," remarked James. "I had to wait for a man with flags to tell me when I could go - it made me very late."

"Ah, but it's not so bad for you," said Gordon importantly. "Your trains don't matter so much, but I've got to pull the Express. You know how the Fat Controller hates to be late."

"Never mind," put in Donald. "Perhaps the wind will be behind you, so that you can go faster and be early. For once," he added cheekily.

Gordon snorted.

"But it would be against me coming back," he objected.

"It might change," suggested Douglas, but he didn't sound very hopeful.

"Pooh!" scoffed Gordon. "I

just wish it would stop whistling around the shed and let an engine get some sleep."

"But it didn't, and the engines were all bleary-eyed and tired when their drivers came next morning. None of them wanted to come out and leave their warm sheds. But they each had a busy day ahead of them on the railway.

Gordon backed on to the coaches of the Express which a shunting engine had taken to the platform for him. He felt cold in spite of his big fire. He waited sulkily for his passengers to climb aboard the train.

At last the Guard blew his whistle and waved his green flag.

"Come along now, come along," Gordon puffed impatiently to the coaches, and moved slowly from the shelter of the station. Suddenly, as the wind hit him, he felt as if he had run into a wall.

"Ooof!" he exclaimed.

"Never mind, Gordon," encouraged his driver. "Keep them moving."

The worst part of the journey was near the Junction, where the gale seemed to whip off the sea with increased fury, blowing gusts of spray. Gordon hated it.

At the station there was a small hut. The workmen used it for storing signal and train lamps and other small odds and ends. Today, as Gordon neared the station, he blinked with astonishment. The hut seemed to

be walking across the platform!

"I must be dreaming," he muttered to himself, but he wasn't, for the driver had seen it too. Quickly he put on the brakes.

"Whoa, Gordon!" he exclaimed. "If we don't stop we shall hit it!"

It was a near thing. Gordon slowed, but bit by bit the hut came closer. Finally, when Gordon was only a few yards off, the hut slid over the edge of the platform. It crashed onto the rails and lay still, right in his path. A moment later with his buffers only inches away, Gordon stopped too.

Porters, inspectors and the Stationmaster all came running.

"Well done, Gordon," said the Stationmaster. "I'm glad you stopped - that might have been a messy accident."

Meanwhile, the porters heaved the battered hut onto a trolley. Then, with much tugging and pulling, they moved it out of Gordon's way so that he could finish his journey.

That day the Express was late, but the Stationmaster explained things to the Fat Controller. As for Gordon, none of the other engines had ever seen a hut that 'walked by itself', and he enjoyed explaining what it looked like.

A PICTURE TO PAINT

THE NAME GAME

What is the hidden name in the grid below? To find out just fill in the names of the characters pictured on the left.

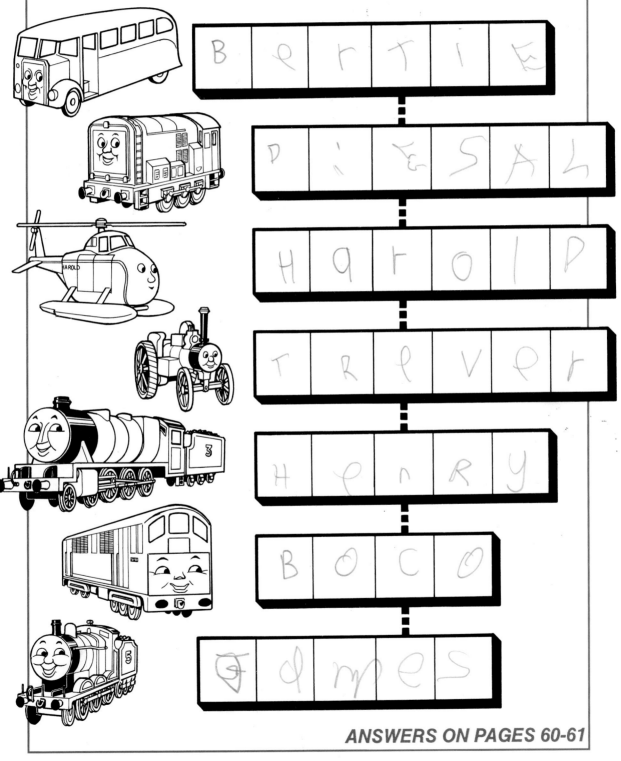

BERTIE

DIESAL

HAROLD

TREVOR

HENRY

BOCO

JAMES

ANSWERS ON PAGES 60-61

53

Bulgy

Oliver

FREE THE ROADS

MAVIS

THE FFARQUHAR QUARRY CO.LTD

Mavis

Can you put the Fat Controller back together?

The Fat Controller is all mixed up! Help him out by putting his matching halves back together again.

1   a

2   b

3   c

4   d

ANSWERS ON PAGES 60-61

SPOT THE DIFFERENCE

Can you find ten things missing in the lower picture?

Page 16
Which Two Pictures Are Identical?
Numbers 3 and 6

Page 21
Which Engine Can Reach The Shed?

Page 30
Spot The Difference

Page 43
Help Bill Find Ben

Page 53
The Name Game
The character names from top to bottom are: Bertie, Diesel, Harold, Trevor, Henry, Boco and James. The hidden name is Terence.

Page 56
Can You Put The Fat Controller Back Together?
1b; 2c; 3d; 4a.

Page 42
**Find
The
Circles**

Page 57
**Spot The
Difference**